# CHRISTINA

## and the Time
## She Quit the Family

by Patricia Lee Gauch

illustrated by Elise Primavera

G. P. Putnam's Sons   New York

# KATERINA

Text copyright © 1987 by Patricia Lee Gauch.
Illustrations copyright © 1987 by Elise Primavera.
All rights reserved. This book, or parts thereof,
may not be reproduced in any form without permission
in writing from the publisher.
G. P. Putnam's Sons, a division of The Putnam & Grosset Group,
200 Madison Avenue, New York, NY 10016.
Sandcastle Books and the Sandcastle logo are trademarks belonging to
The Putnam & Grosset Group.
First Sandcastle Books edition, 1992.
Published simultaneously in Canada.
Printed in Hong Kong by South China Printing Co. (1988) Ltd.
Book design by Alice Lee Groton.

Library of Congress Cataloging-in-Publication Data
Gauch, Patricia Lee.
Christina Katerina and the time she quit the family.
Summary: When Christina quits her family so she can
do whatever she pleases, ignoring her brother and her parents,
she finds total self-reliance can sometimes be lonely.
[1. Self-reliance—Fiction   2. Family life—Fiction.]
I. Primavera, Elise. ill.   II. Title. PZ7.G2315Ck 1987
[E] 86-18658
ISBN 0-399-21408-9 (hardcover)
5   7   9   10   8   6   4
ISBN 0-399-22405-X (Sandcastle)
1   3   5   7   9   10   8   6   4   2
First Sandcastle Books Impression

For CHRISTINE'S MICHAEL—
P.L.G.

For NANETTE STEVENSON—
E.P.

It was a quarter past nine and
a perfectly good Saturday when
Christina Katerina quit the family.

Always before she had liked her family. She liked her mother even though she nagged a little. (Don't lick your fingers, dear. Please don't hum.)

She liked her father even though he grumped. (I need quiet, Christina. No, you can't wear my shoes.)

She even liked her little brother
John who followed her around too
much (into the linen closet, all
around the tub).

But on that perfectly good Saturday at quarter past nine, John and three friends landed in her room, attacking her bears with laser beams and capturing her chair.

Her father came in with his fingers in his ears, shouting, "This time, Christina, you've gone too far!" Her mother ran in behind him, shouting, "This room looks like a war!"

Nobody even knocked.

So, when her mother said, "You just can't do whatever you please when you're part of a family," Christina Katerina quit the family, because doing whatever she pleased sounded just fine to her.

"Call me Agnes," she said.

Her mother said, "All right, Agnes. Call me Mildred. You go your way. We'll go ours."

And Agnes and Mildred divided the house.

Agnes got the left side of the sink, one pile of clean
dishes, one quarter of the living room, three hooks in the
hall, her bedroom and parts of rooms here and there.

Mildred and the family got the right side of the sink, the
cupboard, three quarters of the living room, twelve hooks
in the hall, and the rest of the other rooms here and there.

When they were done dividing, Mildred said "goodbye"
and "have a good time."

Agnes hardly knew where to start.

That night she made a peanut butter and potato chip
sandwich for supper and ate it under the table with three
bears and a hippopotamus who never once said "don't
lick your fingers" or "please don't hum."

And she left her crusts, all of them.

On Sunday she ate under the table whatever she pleased and—she turned one quarter of the living room into a circus. She used the chairs to cage her gorillas, tamed the lion in the fireplace and didn't put anything at all away when she changed her mind and started to play train.

It saved all sorts of time.

On Monday she ate under the table whatever she pleased, played in one quarter of the living room and—wore exactly what she wished to school. Her silky blue flouncy dress. She fixed her hair especially to match, in sweeps and curls on top. And when she couldn't find two blue striped socks to match, she wore one yellow one.

Everything was going just right.

Tuesday Agnes even had a bath alone.
She filled the tub with water up to her
chin and made bubbly towers, and
horses, and hats, and just floated there
until her fingers got warm and wrinkly.
    No one followed her around the tub.
She didn't miss anyone, at all.

Not even on Wednesday.

That day, after she had eaten what she pleased and played where she pleased and dressed as she pleased, she and her orphans decided to stay up all night.

They planned to escape the cruel Miss Shnitzleback's orphanage on the stroke of twelve. But on the stroke of eleven, they ran into a Something

...near the stairs

...that appeared to move

which Agnes would have liked to ask Mildred about.

Only Mildred was asleep.

So was Father.

And John.

But Agnes very suddenly got sleepy anyway and disappeared by the stroke of twelve.

True, on Thursday John was standing right there when Agnes was creating her Surprise Soufflé. It might have helped if, while she was stirring eggs and ginger ale, he had handed her the pepper. Or the apples.

She might not have reached for them. And tripped on the broom. And broken the bowl. And knocked over the garbage. And let the dog out.

"I don't know any Agnes," John said.

And it might have been pleasant on Friday to have
found just one clean dish in the "Agnes" pile or shared
a piece of the chocolate cake on the "Mildred" side of
the sink or had someone to help her wind her yarn in
the one quarter of the living room.

(The chair was quiet but no help at all.)

No one even noticed.

On Friday she decided to be Agnes forever.

It was at bedtime. The others were in John's room laughing and eating the Mildred-side chocolate cake and telling stories, nice and loud at the beginning and in whispers at the end.

Not that Agnes heard them.

She was far too busy tucking herself in. The bears were no help. Neither was the hippopotamus.

If she kept one arm out to tuck with, that arm got cold. If she kneeled and pulled the blanket over her head, she couldn't breathe. Finally, she rolled, first to this side, then to that, and…it worked.

"Perfectly tucked!" she said right out loud.

"I CERTAINLY DON'T NEED ANYONE AROUND HERE," she went on.

"THAT'S FOR SURE!" she added.

"NOTHING BETTER THAN DOING WHAT I PLEASE!"

But there was silence.

That was the exact moment when she shouted, "I'M GOING TO BE AGNES FOREVER!"

And she would have, except for poor Mildred.

She knocked on the door and tiptoed in.

"Agnes," she said, "please eat this end piece of cake. Everyone else hates so much frosting."

After all, Mildred did say please.

"And Agnes, would you tell John a story? He only wants a blood-curdling one."

It was true. No one could curdle blood like she could.

"And then, Agnes, would you keep your father company? It's been so quiet, he says he hasn't been able to work."

Keeping her father company always was what she did best.

That night, after she had finished off the cake, told John a blood-curdling story, and kept her father good company, she finally crawled back into bed and—with a little help—tucked herself in.

A few moments later Mildred called from down the hall.

"Good night, Agnes," she said.

"Call me Christina," Agnes shouted back.

"Call me Mother, Christina," Mildred shouted back.

And Christina did, because Christina liked doing what she pleased, and that's exactly what pleased her just then.